P9-CQW-232

6
7
8
9
10

3...

MARGARET K. McELDERRY BOOKS
An imprint of Simon & Schuster Children's Publishing Division
1230 Avenue of the Americas, New York, New York 10020

Originally published in Great Britain by Hodder Children's Books, a division of Hachette Children's Group

Book design by Ann Bobco
The text for this book was set in P22Garamouche.
Manufactured in China
0817 HCB
First Edition
10 9 8 7 6 5 4 3 2 1
CIP data for this book is available from the Library of Congress.
ISBN 978-1-5344-0014-6
ISBN 978-1-5344-0015-3 (eBook)

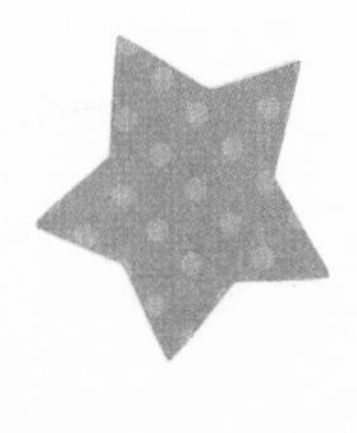

Ellie ☆ Sandall

EVERYBUNNY Count!

4...

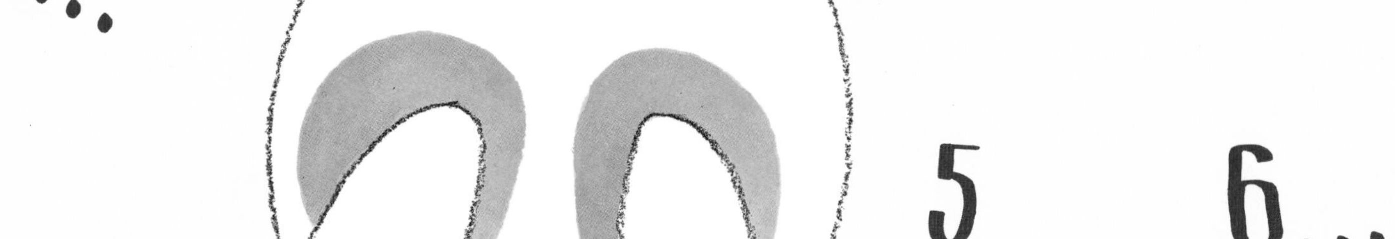

5... 6... 7...

Margaret K. McElderry Books
New York • London • Toronto • Sydney • New Delhi

Fox and bunnies like to play,
all together, every day.

Playing **hide**-and-**seek** today...

EVERYBUNNY COUNT!

6
7
8
9
10

Take your places, everyone.
Ready or not, here we come!

The search for fox has just begun.
Everybunny count to **ONE**!

We found some birds, away they flew.
Everybunny count to **TWO!**

We've spotted something in the tree.
Everybunny count to THREE!

Tiny creatures in my paw.
Everybunny count to **FOUR!**

Check the water, in we dive.
Everybunny count to FIVE!

Look who's hiding in the sticks.
Everybunny count to **SIX**!

Carrots! We're in bunny heaven.
Everybunny count to **SEVEN!**

Where's that fox? It's getting late.
Everybunny count to **EIGHT!**

Sleepy bunnies in a line.

Everybunny count to NINE!

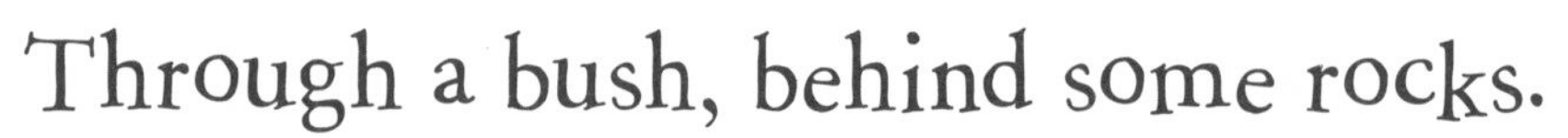

Through a bush, behind some rocks.

Everybunny look...

...it's **FOX!**

Now take a peek inside the den.

EVERYBUNNY
COUNT...

TO TEN!

Foxes, bunnies,

one to ten.

Let's play **hide**-and-**seek** again!

1
2
3
4
5